info buzz

Neil Armstrong

Izzi Howell

W

FRANKLIN WATTS
LONDON • SYDNEY

Franklin Watts
First published in Great Britain in 2018 by The Watts Publishing Group
Copyright © The Watts Publishing Group, 2018

Produced for Franklin Watts by
White-Thomson Publishing Ltd
www.wtpub.co.uk

ISBN: 978 1 4451 5948 5
10 9 8 7 6 5 4 3 2 1

Credits
Series Editor: Izzi Howell
Series Designer: Rocket Design (East Anglia) Ltd
Designer: Clare Nicholas
Literacy Consultant: Kate Ruttle

The publisher would like to thank the following for permission to reproduce their pictures: Alamy: ITAR-TASS Photo Agency 8; DRC University of Cincinnati, Armstrong, Neil, 1930-2012; United States. Office of the Chief of Naval Operations 7t; Getty: csfotoimages 6, Joyce Naltchayan/AFP 20; NASA: *cover, title page,* 5, 9, 10, 11, 12, 13, 14t, 14b, 16, 17 and 18, Bill Taub 19, David Scott 21; Shutterstock: Klagyivik Viktor 4, MarcelClemens 15; U.S. Navy Naval Aviation News 7b.

Every attempt has been made to clear copyright. Should there be any inadvertent omission please apply to the publisher for rectification.

Printed in China

Franklin Watts
An imprint of
Hachette Children's Group
Part of The Watts Publishing Group
Carmelite House
50 Victoria Embankment
London EC4Y 0DZ

An Hachette UK Company
www.hachette.co.uk
www.franklinwatts.co.uk

All words in **bold** appear in the glossary on page 23.

Contents

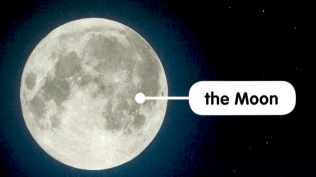

the Moon

Who was Neil Armstrong?

Neil Armstrong was an **astronaut**. In 1969, he was the first person to walk on the Moon.

▲

The Moon is in space. It is far away from where we live on Earth.

Neil Armstrong travelled to the Moon with two other astronauts. Their **mission** was called Apollo 11.

The Moon is over 380,000 **kilometres** from Earth.

▼ The Apollo 11 astronauts

Michael Collins

Neil Armstrong

Buzz Aldrin

Growing up

Neil Armstrong was born on
5 August 1930 in Ohio,
in the United States
of America (USA).
He loved planes
when he was a child.

Neil was born here.

USA

▼ Neil flew in a plane
like this when he
was six years old.

Have you ever flown in a plane?

Neil learned how to fly a plane when he was sixteen years old. He flew planes for the **US Navy**.

Neil wore a uniform in the US Navy. ▶

Neil Armstrong's plane

The Space Race

In the 1950s, the Space Race was a race to send the first person into space. The USA and Russia both wanted to win the Space Race.

▶ In 1961, Russia sent the first person into space. His name was Yuri Gagarin.

The USA still wanted to beat Russia. They asked **NASA** to work out how to send astronauts to the Moon.

▲ NASA astronauts learned how to leave a **spacecraft** and float in space.

Neil and NASA

Neil Armstrong worked for NASA in the 1950s. He tested planes to make sure they were safe to fly.

▼ Neil flew over 200 different types of planes for NASA.

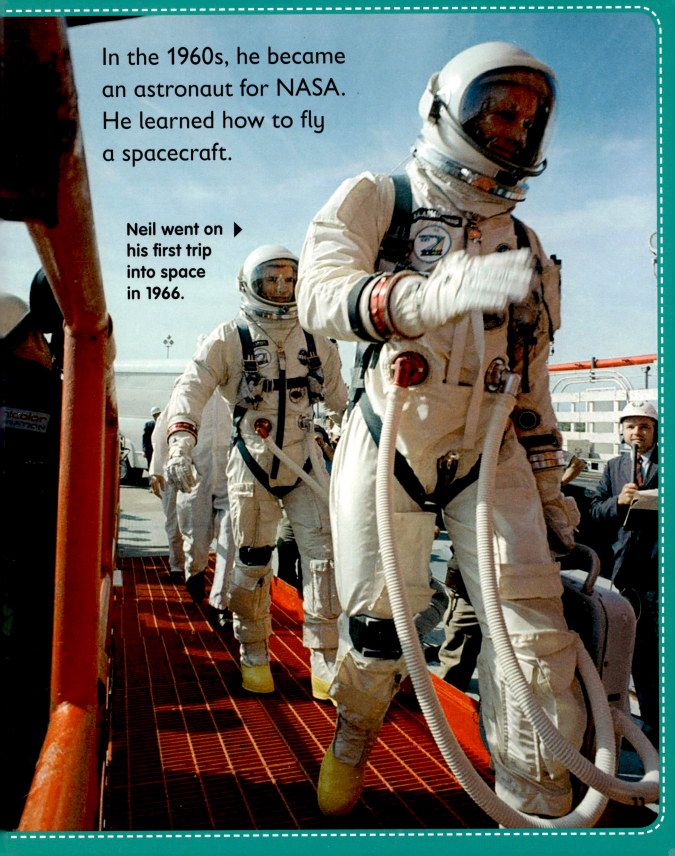

In the 1960s, he became an astronaut for NASA. He learned how to fly a spacecraft.

Neil went on ▶ his first trip into space in 1966.

Space training

In 1969, NASA was ready for a mission to the Moon. They asked Neil, Buzz and Michael to go.

◀ The astronauts practised wearing their spacesuits before they left.

No one had been to the Moon before. It was dangerous. But Neil and the other astronauts were **brave**.

Would you like to travel into space?

▲ The Apollo 11 astronauts smiled as they went into the rocket.

Lift off!

On 16 July 1969, Neil Armstrong and the other astronauts left Earth in a spacecraft. A rocket carried the spacecraft up into space.

◀ The Apollo 11 rocket went up into the sky after **lift off**.

◀ The rocket travelled up towards the Moon.

What sound do you think the rocket made?

The Apollo 11 astronauts saw Earth from the window of their spacecraft. ▼

It took four days for the spacecraft to reach the Moon. Michael waited in a part of the spacecraft in **orbit**. Neil and Buzz flew another part of the spacecraft down to the Moon.

Walking on the Moon

Neil Armstrong left the spacecraft first. When he stepped on the Moon, he said, 'That's one small step for (a) man, one giant leap for mankind'.

The astronauts wore spacesuits that helped them to breathe. ▶

How do you think Neil Armstrong felt when he walked on the Moon?

Neil and Buzz explored
the Moon for over two hours.
They collected soil and rocks
to bring back to Earth.

▼ The astronauts
put the flag of
the USA on
the Moon.

Back to Earth

The astronauts joined Michael in space. Then they flew back to Earth in part of the spacecraft. They landed in the ocean.

▼ People came in a boat to help the astronauts leave the spacecraft.

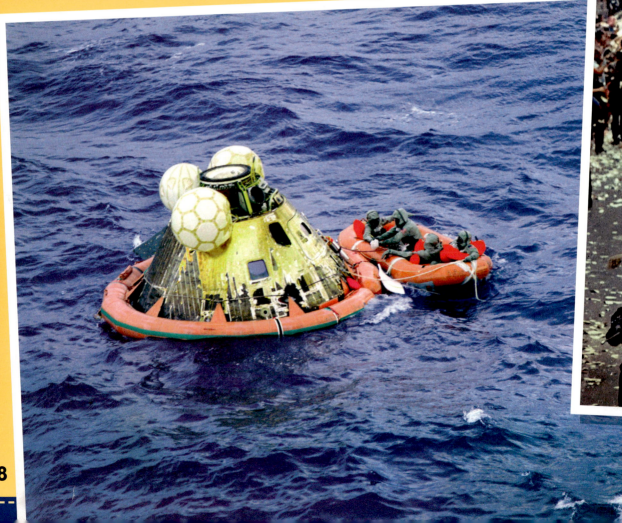

18

The Apollo 11 trip to the Moon
made people very excited.
The USA had beaten Russia.

▼ Neil Armstrong and
the other astronauts
rode in a **parade** to
welcome them home.

Have you
seen a parade?
What was it
celebrating?

Later years

After his trip to the Moon, Neil Armstrong was **famous**. He was given awards and medals for his hard work and **bravery**.

▲ **Michael Collins, Neil Armstrong and Buzz Aldrin show their medals.**

Neil Armstrong died in 2012. He was 82 years old. We will always remember him as the first person to walk on the Moon.

▲ Other astronauts went to the Moon after Apollo 11. They drove a **rover** and explored.

Quiz

Test how much you remember.

Check your answers on page 24.

1 When was Neil born?

2 Who was Yuri Gagarin?

3 When did Neil go into space for the first time?

4 How long did it take for the spacecraft to travel to the Moon?

5 Where did the spacecraft land on Earth?

6 How old was Neil Armstrong when he died?

Glossary

astronaut – someone who travels into space

brave – not being afraid to do something scary

bravery – doing scary things without showing that you are afraid

famous – known by lots of people

kilometre – a distance of 1,000 metres

lift off – when a rocket leaves the ground and travels up into the air

mission – an important job that involves travelling somewhere

NASA – a US organisation that studies space travel and exploration (National Aeronautics and Space Administration)

Navy – ships, sailors and planes that fight in wars

orbit – circling around the Earth, the Sun or another planet

parade – a line of people who walk somewhere to celebrate something

rover – a small vehicle that can travel on rough ground

spacecraft – a vehicle that can travel into space

US – from the United States of America

Index

Answers:

1: 1930; 2: The first person to travel into space; 3: 1966; 4: Four days; 5: In the ocean; 6: 82 years old

Teaching notes:

Children who are reading Book band Purple or above should be able to enjoy this book with some independence. Other children will need more support.

Before you share the book:

- What do the children already know about the Moon landing? Do they know the names of any of the astronauts?
- Show children an image of the Earth and Moon in space. Talk about the fact that the Moon goes around (orbits) the Earth.

While you share the book:

- Help children to read some of the more unfamiliar words.
- Talk about the questions. Encourage children to make links between their own experiences and the Moon landing.

- Discuss the information about Neil Armstrong's early life. Can they guess why he wanted to fly a plane?
- Talk about the pictures. How can you tell that some of the pictures were taken a long time ago?

After you have shared the book:

- Talk about the spacecraft. Compare the huge rocket that took off (see page 14) with the little spacecraft that landed back in the ocean (see page 18).
- Ask children to find out from their grandparents about their memories of the Moon landing.
- Talk about other missions to the Moon and when the last one took place.
- Work through the free activity sheets at www.hachetteschools.co.uk

History

978 1 4451 5948 5

Who was
Neil Armstrong?
Growing up
The Space Race
Neil and NASA
Space training
Lift off!
Walking on the Moon
Back to Earth
Later years

978 1 4451 5886 0

Who is
Queen Elizabeth II?
What does the
Queen do?
Around the world
Childhood
Marriage and children
Becoming Queen
The royal family
Special days
At home

978 1 4451 5950 8

Who was
Queen Victoria?
Childhood
Becoming Queen
Marriage and children
Around the world
Sad times
Change
Later years
Remembering Victoria

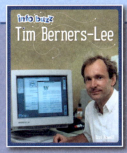

978 1 4451 5952 2

Who is
Tim Berners-Lee?
Childhood
University
A new job
Back to CERN
The World Wide Web
Across the world
The Web today
After the Web

Religion

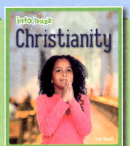

978 1 4451 5962 1

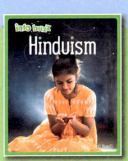

978 1 4451 5964 5

978 1 4451 5968 3

978 1 4451 5966 9

Countries

978 1 4451 5958 4

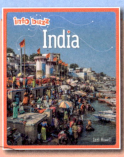

978 1 4451 5960 7

978 1 4451 5956 0

978 1 4451 5954 6

Franklin WATTS